In memory of my dear mom, Alexine Wallace. —N. E. W.
In memory of my dear grandpa Lu. —A. L.

Library of Congress Cataloging-in-Publication Data available.

ISBN 978-1-4521-8156-1

Manufactured in China.

MIX
Paper from
responsible sources
FSC™ C104723
FSC
www.fsc.org

Design by Mariam Quraishi.
Typeset in Catalina Clemente.
Interior handlettering by Kayla Lewis.
The illustrations in this book were rendered in mixed media.

10 9 8 7 6 5 4 3 2 1

Chronicle Books LLC
680 Second Street
San Francisco, California 94107

Chronicle Books—we see things differently.
Become part of our community at www.chroniclekids.com.

Can Sophie Change the World?

Written by
Nancy Elizabeth Wallace

Illustrated by
Aura Lewis

chronicle books · san francisco

It was a normal Sunday afternoon except for one thing.
"Grandpop, your birthday's in only one week!"
Sophie was very excited. "What can I give you?"

"Hmmm," said Grandpop. "I have everything I need.
I really don't need more."
"Something, Grandpop!" said Sophie.

Grandpop thought for a minute. "I know!" he said. "You could change the world!"
"Change the WORLD! How?" asked Sophie.
"By doing kind deeds! Give me a mitzvah, a kind deed!" Grandpop said.
"More than anything, that's what I want."

That night Sophie was worried.
The world was so big!
How could she change it?
She didn't know.
But she would try.

On Monday Sophie shared her puppets with Ben,
taught Ayesha the clapping song, and
asked the new student, Evan, to play catch.

Sophie liked being a friend.
But, she thought, *I didn't change the world.*

On Tuesday, when Sophie saw cans on the grass, she picked them up and dropped them in the recycle bin.

When a baby dropped her stuffed animal, Sophie ran to return it.

Sophie liked helping.
But, she thought,
I didn't change the world.

On Wednesday she filled her family's empty birdbath and watered her neighbor's wilting flowers.

Sophie liked taking care of things.

But, she thought,
I didn't change the world.

On Thursday Sophie played with
Sari so Mom could paint.
That made Mom smile and Sophie, too.

But, she thought, *I didn't change the world.*

On Friday Sophie worked with Mom and Dad in the community garden. Sophie liked giving some of the vegetables she helped grow to people who needed them.

Still, she thought,
I didn't change the world.

This garden
helps feed
those in
need

When Sophie got to Grandpop's on the weekend, she ran to him. "Grandpop, I tried! I did lots of mitzvahs! I *really* tried, but I couldn't change the world. I really wanted to."

Grandpop looked at her very seriously. "Tell me about your mitzvahs."

When she finished, Grandpop's eyes were twinkling. "Sweetheart, every mitzvah, every act of kindness, big or small, makes a difference.

"If you hadn't invited Evan to play, he would have felt left out. What if you hadn't found the baby's stuffed animal? She might not have been able to sleep without it.

"And watering your neighbor's wilted flowers, well, that was a double mitzvah!"

"A double mitzvah?"

"Yes! You kept the flowers alive and blooming by giving them a good, long drink of water, and you helped your neighbor by watering her flowers while she was away."

Sophie was quiet.

Grandpop gave her a big, warm, snuggle hug. "Acts of kindness, big or small, are how you change the world. Do you see that your kindness made our world a more giving, sharing, blooming, caring place?"

Suddenly she did.

And then Sophie had an idea.

First they cut out shapes.
Then Grandpop glued while Sophie wrote.
They worked together.

playing
my little

"Happy birthday, Grandpop!"

making a
new friend

Sharing my
puppets

Playing with
my friends

with
ster

Watering
flowers

Working in
the garden

ling

roll back to
the baby

giving birds
a drink

helping my
neighbor

"This is a perfect birthday gift," said Grandpop.
"You and your mitzvahs make me so happy!"

Sophie felt happy, too.
She wanted to do more and more and more mitzvahs.

Now Sophie knew how to change the world!

Author's note

When I was growing up, my mom was my role model for being caring and kind. She was ALWAYS looking to see if someone needed help, a meal delivered, a listening ear, or to be included. When I feel helpless and get to worrying about *how I can change our world to make it better*, I remember my mom showing me that even a small act of kindness can make a BIG difference to someone else—and in the doing, my own heart becomes happier, too!
Thank you, Mom, for your lasting gift!